THE ULTIMATE
Meerkat
BOOK *for* KIDS

BELLANOVA

MELBOURNE · SOFIA · BERLIN

Copyright © 2026 by Jenny Kellett
Meerkats: The Ultimate Meerkat Book for Kids

Visit us at:
www.bellanovabooks.com

All rights reserved. No part of this book may be reproduced in any form by any electronic or mechanical means including photocopying, recording, or information storage and retrieval without permission in writing from the author.

Imprint: Bellanova Books
ISBN: 978-619-264-007-1

Contents

Introduction	4
Let's Meet the Meerkat Family	6
Meerkat anatomy	8
Where Meerkats Live	10
Life in the Kalahari	12
The Life of a Meerkat	14
A day in the life of a meerkat	16
Where meerkats rest and roam	18
The Meerkat Mob	20
Meerkat pups	24
Talk of the mob	28
Diet & Hunting	30
Meerkats in the food chain	32
What's for dinner?	34
Foraging techniques	36
Protecting Meerkats	38
Endangered or safe?	40
Are meerkats safe?	42
What can you do to help?	44
Meerkat Fun Facts	46
The Meerkat Quiz	64
Answers	68
Meerkat Word Search	70
Solution	72
Sources	73
Also by Jenny Kellett	77

Introduction

WELCOME TO THE FAST-PACED WORLD OF MEERKATS!

They're famously cute and curious, but there's so much more to meerkats than that! Did you know they are some of the best team players in the animal kingdom? And that they are as smart as dolphins?

These gorgeous creatures are truly fascinating and we have a lot to learn from them. In this book you'll learn what makes them so special and have a chance to test your newfound knowledge at the end.

Are you ready? Let's go!

DID YOU KNOW?

Meerkats are often called Suricates.

Let's Meet the Meerkat Family

Meerkats are fascinating creatures that live in the arid regions of southern Africa. They belong to a single species, **Suricata suricatta**, and are known for their social behavior and incredible adaptability to harsh environments.

Desert Survival

Meerkats are perfectly adapted to their harsh desert habitats. Their burrows keep them cool during the hot days and warm during the chilly nights.

Meerkats are also experts at conserving water. They rarely drink water, getting the hydration they need from the food they eat.

Regional Differences

While all meerkats belong to the same species, those living in different regions may have slight variations in behavior and appearance. For example, meerkats in the **Namib Desert** may have lighter fur to blend into their sandy environment better.

Meerkats can dig through sand equivalent to their body weight in just seconds! This helps them create extensive underground networks to escape from predators quickly.

Smart ears

Their large, rounded ears can be closed when digging to keep dirt out.

Long, slender body

The meerkat's body is lean and agile, allowing it to maneuver through tight spaces in its burrow and quickly chase after prey like insects.

Meerkat Anatomy

Thin fur
Meerkats have short, coarse fur to help them cope with the harsh desert climate.

Sharp claws
Meerkats have long, strong claws that allow them to dig burrows quickly.

Tail for Balance
Their tails are not bushy but rather long and slender, used mostly for balance while standing upright.

Meerkats are designed for survival.

Each part of their body is perfectly designed to help them thrive in their tough desert environment.

From their sharp claws for digging to their smart ears that can pick up the slightest sounds, every feature has a special role.

The Life of a *Meerkat*

Ever wondered what a day in the life of a meerkat looks like? Meerkats are lively and social animals who lead exciting lives filled with foraging, playing, and guarding their territory. In this chapter, we'll dive into the daily activities that keep meerkats busy in the wild!

A Day in the Life of a Meerkat

Meerkats have busy lives! From the moment they wake up, meerkats are on the move, exploring their territories, playing with their friends, or resting together.

Meerkats take turns standing guard while the others forage or play. They use different calls to alert their group of approaching danger.

Foraging

As the sun rises, meerkats emerge from their burrows to start their day. They spread out to forage for food, digging for insects, small mammals, and even scorpions.

Resting

After a busy morning of foraging and playing, meerkats often rest during the hottest part of the day. They find a shaded area or return to their burrows to nap and conserve energy.

Playing

Afternoons and evenings are often for playing and grooming each other. This helps strengthen their bonds and keep their fur clean.

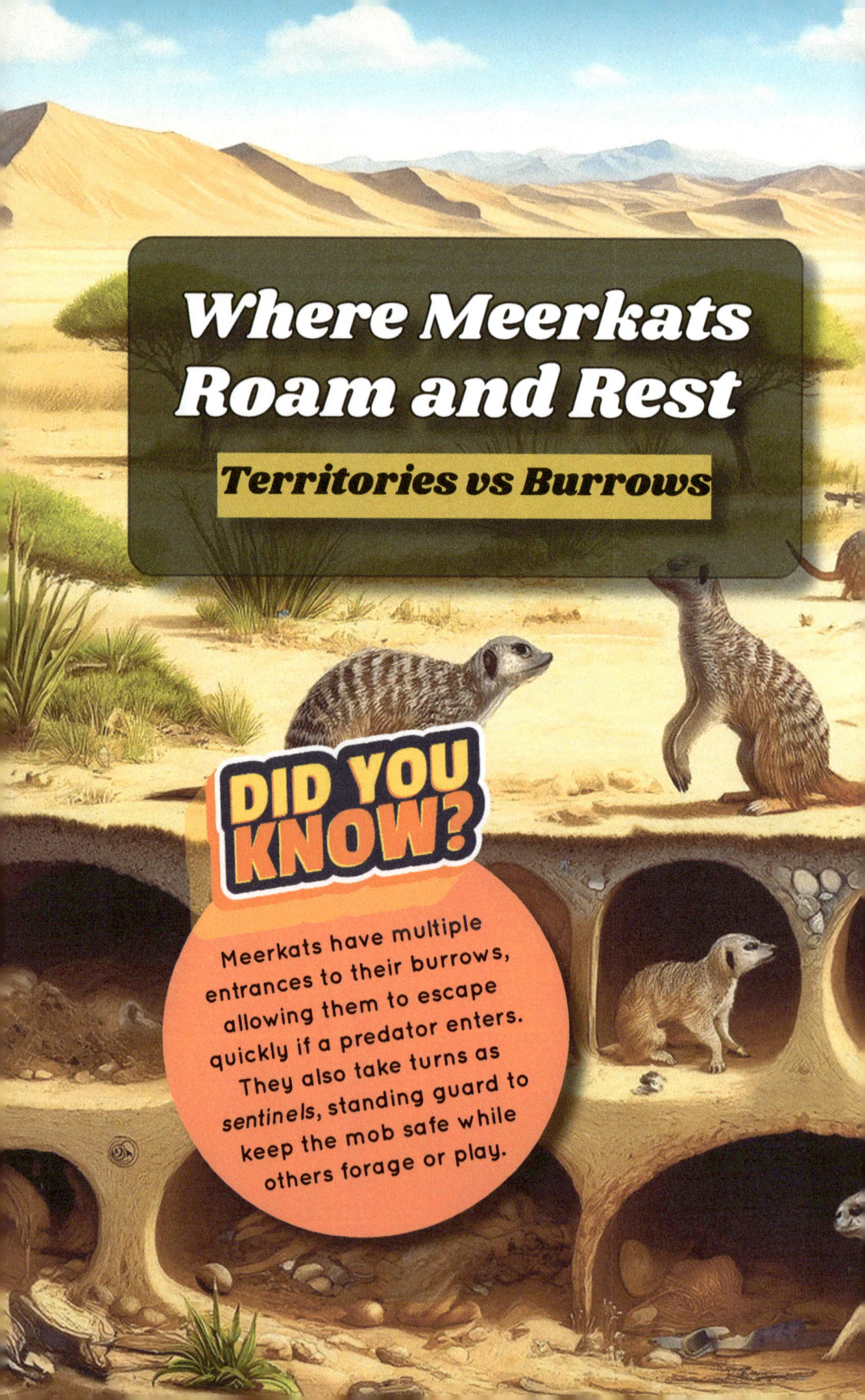

Where Meerkats Roam and Rest
Territories vs Burrows

DID YOU KNOW?

Meerkats have multiple entrances to their burrows, allowing them to escape quickly if a predator enters. They also take turns as sentinels, standing guard to keep the mob safe while others forage or play.

The Burrow: A Safe Haven

Meerkat burrows are intricate networks of tunnels and chambers, providing a safe home for the whole mob. These burrows are usually located in open areas where meerkats can easily spot approaching predators.

Burrows are cool retreats from the scorching desert sun, and they offer protection from predators. Meerkats sleep, raise their young, and escape from extreme weather in these underground homes.

The Territory: Shared Space

A meerkat mob's territory can cover a wide area, which they patrol and defend against other meerkat groups. This territory includes multiple burrows, foraging grounds, and lookout points.

Territories are vital for a mob's survival, providing access to food, water, and safe places to live. Meerkats work together to maintain and defend their territory from intruders.

The Meerkat Mob

A meerkat mob is a big family of meerkats that live and work together. There can be up to 50 meerkats in a mob!

Living in a mob helps meerkats stay safe and find food more easily. Each meerkat has an important job to do, and they all work together to take care of each other. This teamwork helps them survive in the wild deserts where they live.

THE ALPHA PAIR

At the top of the mob are the alpha male and alpha female. They are the leaders of the group. The alpha female is usually the one who decides where the mob goes and when they move. She is also the only female in the mob who has babies.

THE BABYSITTERS

Not all meerkats have babies, but everyone helps take care of them! Some meerkats stay behind to babysit the pups, while others go out to look for food. Babysitters make sure the pups are safe and teach them how to be meerkats.

THE LOOKOUTS

Meerkats are always on the lookout for danger. Some meerkats stand guard while the others search for food. The lookouts climb to a high spot and watch for predators like eagles and snakes. If they see danger, they bark loudly to warn the others.

THE HUNTERS AND GATHERERS

Most of the meerkats go out each day to hunt for food. They dig in the ground for insects, lizards, and scorpions. Meerkats are very good at finding food and share what they find with the rest of the mob.

Meerkat Pups

Meerkat pups are born tiny, blind, and completely helpless, but they quickly grow into curious and playful young meerkats.

Each litter usually has 2 to 5 pups, born in a cozy burrow deep underground. For the first two weeks of their lives, they stay hidden, safe from predators and the harsh desert sun.

First Steps

At around **three weeks old**, the pups are ready to explore outside the burrow. This is an exciting time as they take their first wobbly steps into the sunlight, always under the watchful eyes of babysitters.

DID YOU KNOW?

Meerkat pups are incredibly vocal. They use a variety of sounds to communicate with their family members, from tiny peeps and chirps to louder calls that signal danger.

Learning the Ropes

Pups learn by watching and mimicking adults. They play-fight with each other, developing hunting and defense skills. Adults also teach them how to dig for insects and scorpions and remove scorpion stingers safely.

Becoming Independent

As they grow older, the pups become more adventurous and join adults on short foraging trips. By three months old, they start learning how to find food on their own, practicing digging for insects and small animals.

The Importance of Play

Play is crucial for a meerkat pup's development. Through play-fighting and mock hunting, they learn interaction, build strength, and develop the agility needed for survival. The games mimic real-life scenarios, preparing them for adulthood.

Growing Up Fast

Meerkat pups grow quickly. Within a few months, they are nearly the size of the adults, though they still have a lot to learn. They continue to rely on older meerkats for guidance until they can look after themselves.

Ready for the Future

By one year old, meerkat pups are ready for adult responsibilities! Some stay with their birth group, while others join new mobs.

Talk of the Mob

Meerkats have their own special way of talking to each other! They use different sounds and body movements to share information. This helps them stay connected with their mob and keep everyone safe.

A meerkat's **chirp** can tell the mob if there's food nearby or if there's danger! A quick chirp might mean, *"Look out, there's an eagle!"* while a softer chirp could mean, *"I found something yummy!"*

Meerkats **whistle** to call other mob members. These whistles can be heard far away and help keep the group together. When a meerkat hears a whistle, they know it's time to come home!

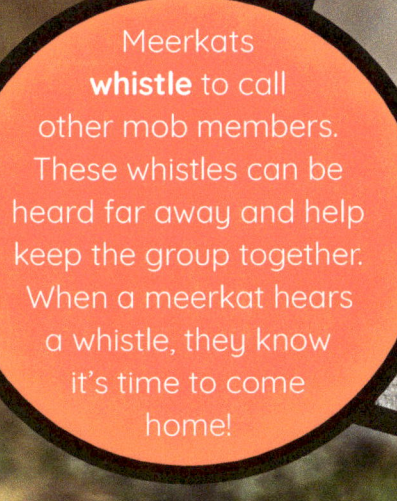

Meerkats make over 30 DIFFERENT SOUNDS? Each one means something different and helps the mob stay organized.

Meerkats also use **body language** to communicate. When a meerkat stands tall on its hind legs, it's keeping watch for danger. If it suddenly ducks down, the others know to hide quickly.

Where Meerkats Live

Meerkats live in some of the driest and hottest places on Earth! Their favorite habitats are the deserts and grasslands of southern Africa.

Let's explore where they call home!

Meerkats are found in countries like **South Africa, Botswana, Namibia, and Angola.** These places have large, open areas with lots of sunshine and not much rain.

Life in the Kalahari

One of the most famous places where meerkats live is the Kalahari Desert. This huge desert covers parts of Botswana, Namibia, and South Africa. It's a tough place to live, but meerkats have adapted perfectly.

LIFE OF EXTREMES

HOT DAYS, COLD NIGHTS: The Kalahari can be extremely hot during the day and very cold at night.

SANDY DUNES: The landscape is full of sandy dunes and rocky areas where meerkats can find insects and other food.

Meerkats have special adaptations that help them live in such a harsh environment, including dark circles around their eyes that act like sunglasses and super tough paws that can walk on the hot sand.

SURVIVING THE SEASONS

The weather in meerkat habitats can change dramatically. During the dry season, water is scarce, and food can be hard to find. But meerkats are resourceful and know how to survive.

- **RAINY SEASON:** When it does rain, plants grow quickly, and there's plenty of food.
- **DRY SEASON:** Meerkats rely on the water stored in the plants they eat and dig deeper to find hidden insects.

Diet & Hunting

Meerkats are **omnivores**, meaning they eat both plants and animals. So how do they find their food? Meerkats are skilled **foragers** that use their sharp senses to find tasty treats in the wild. Let's find out more!

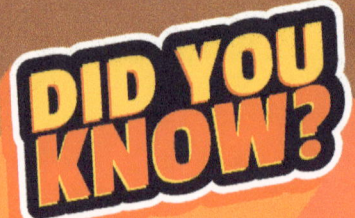

Meerkats have an incredible sense of smell - and long noses - that help them sniff out insects and other small animals hidden underground.

Meerkats in the Food Chain

Meerkats play a crucial role in their ecosystem. By eating insects and small animals, they help control pest populations and keep the environment balanced.

> Meerkats eat many small animals but are also prey for larger predators, so they must always be alert!

Venomous snakes

Birds of prey

Jackals

Meerkat Predators

The Energy Starter
The sun provides energy to plants, which is the first step in the food chain.

The Producers
Plants use sunlight to grow and are eaten by many animals.

The Predator
Meerkats eat insects and small animals to get their energy and help keep the population in check.

The Plant Eaters
Herbivores eat plants to get their energy.

The Recyclers
Tiny creatures in the soil break down waste and dead animals, returning nutrients to the earth.

Can you think of another predator that plays a key role in the food chain?

What's for dinner, Mr. Meerkat?!

Meerkats are not picky eaters! They love munching on insects, but they also eat small mammals, birds, and even plants. Their diet changes with the seasons and what they can find in their habitat.

Insects

Meerkats love to eat beetles, termites, and scorpions. They skillfully remove the stingers from scorpions before eating them.

Small Animals

Mice, small birds, and lizards are also on the meerkat menu.

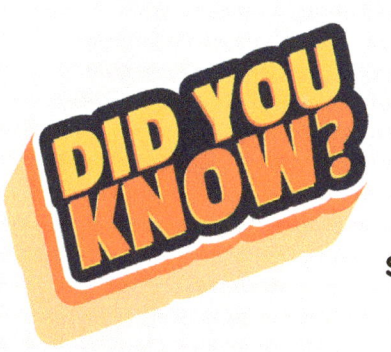

Approximately 82 per cent of a meerkat's diet is insects. Their next favorite meal is spiders, followed by centipedes. Yum!

Fruits & Plants

Sometimes, meerkats munch on fruits and vegetables, especially when other food is scarce.

Foraging Techniques

Meerkats are skilled foragers who use teamwork and smart strategies to find food. Let's explore some of their clever techniques!

The Teaching Role

Older meerkats teach the younger ones how to find and catch food. This important role ensures that every meerkat knows how to forage successfully.

The Lookout

One meerkat always stands guard while the others forage. The lookout keeps an eye out for danger and warns the group with a special call if a predator is near.

The Scent Hunters

Meerkats use their long noses to sniff out hidden insects and small animals.

Meerkats use their sharp claws to dig in the ground for insects, grubs, and other tasty treats.

Protecting Meerkats

CONSERVATION

Conservation is all about protecting our planet's amazing animals and the places they call home. Just like we need a cozy house to live in, animals like meerkats need safe places to roam, hunt, and raise their pups. Although meerkats are not currently endangered, they face challenges that could threaten their survival in the future.

But don't worry, there are ways that *you* can help!

Did you know...

Conservationists use a special list to keep track of how animals are doing. When an animal is in danger of vanishing from the wild, it is called 'Endangered'.

ENDANGERED OR SAFE?

Let's explore the journey of wildlife conservation! Look at the path below. Just like in a game, animals can move up and down this path depending on how safe they are in the wild. Our actions can help them stay away from the danger zone of 'Extinct'.

EXTINCT

Golden toad

Hawaiian crow

EXTINCT IN THE WILD

Amur leopard

CRITICALLY ENDANGERED

Did you know...
9,760 animals are currently listed as critically endangered!

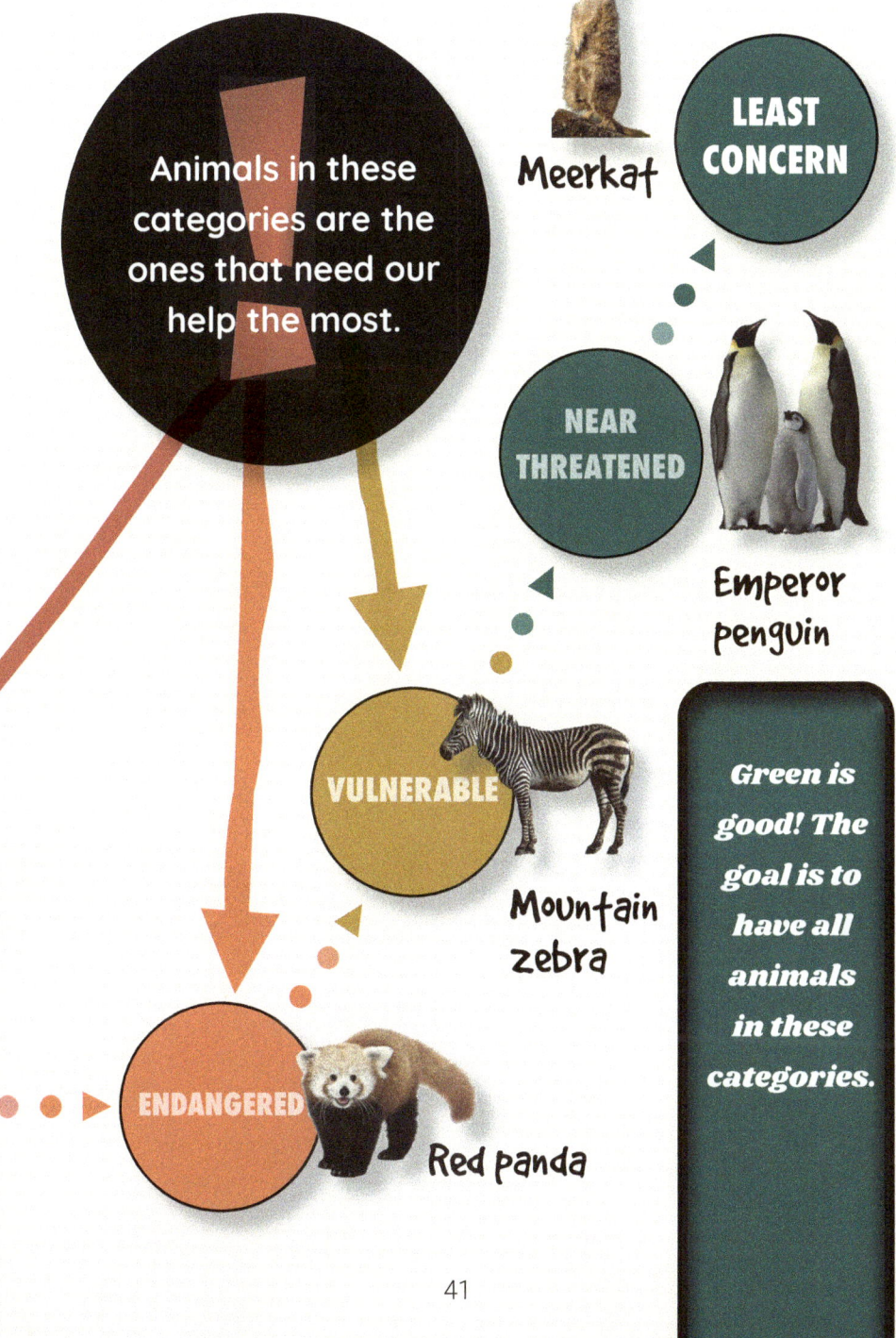

Are Meerkats Safe?

Habitat Loss

Fortunately, much of the area that meerkats call home is in protected areas around the **Kalahari desert,** which protects them from many dangers that other animals face, such as habitat loss. However, this may not always be the case. As towns and farms expand, meerkats continue to lose their natural homes.

> *Even though meerkats are not currently endangered, protecting their habitat is crucial to ensure they continue to thrive.*

Climate Change

Climate change can affect the availability of food and water in meerkat habitats. Droughts can make it harder for meerkats to find insects and small animals.

DID YOU KNOW?

Climate change can impact meerkat populations by reducing the availability of food and water, making it harder for them to survive.

A helping hand

Conservationists are protecting natural habitats by planting trees, creating wildlife corridors, and removing roads to give meerkats the space they need.

What can you do to help?

Everyone can play a role in ensuring a safe future for meerkats and their neighbors.

Here are some ways you can contribute to their conservation and become a true Meerkat Hero!

Share your knowledge

Tell your friends and family about what you've learned about meerkats. The more people know about meerkats, the more they'll want to help!

Conservation Challenge!

Keep a **conservation diary** this week and write down any action you take that helps the environment, like recycling, saving water, or learning about local wildlife.

Visit a wildlife sanctuary

Support meerkat conservation by visiting a wildlife sanctuary. Your visit can help fund the care and protection of meerkats and other animals.

Everyday actions make a difference!

By recycling, using less water, and reducing waste, you can help conserve natural resources and reduce pollution, which indirectly supports the preservation of meerkat habitats and the overall health of our planet.

Support conservation groups

Many organizations work hard to protect meerkats. You can help by raising money with a bake sale, volunteering, or even adopting a meerkat online!

Meerkat Fun Facts

You've already learned so much about meerkats, but there's still much more to discover! Prepare to dive into a treasure trove of even more fascinating and fun facts about meerkats.

Meerkats love sunbathing and stand on their hind legs to soak up the morning sun.

• • •

Meerkats are immune to many different venomous snakes and insects!

• • •

Meerkats take turns playing lookout to spot danger and keep everyone safe.

When confronted with predators, meerkats exhibit mobbing behavior where the group bands together to intimidate and drive away the threat. They will puff up their fur, hiss, and even attack in a coordinated manner.

• • •

They can close their ears to keep out dirt while digging—pretty handy, huh?

• • •

Their fur helps them stay toasty warm at night and cool during the day.

• • •

Young meerkats sometimes cry wolf just to see everyone scramble—sneaky!

Meerkats often hide in tall grass while hunting for food. The grass provides protection from predators.

Meerkats often cuddle in a circle with their tails touching to catch some Z's.

• • •

Studies found that meerkats are almost as smart as animals such as chimps, dolphins and even humans when completing complex tasks!

• • •

Meerkats love grooming each other to stay clean and show they care.

• • •

Meerkats sometimes get fascinated by their own reflections in shiny objects.

• • •

Mobs move to new burrows every few months to keep things fresh and safe.

Meerkats have secret food stashes hidden away for when they have a day when they can't find fresh food.

• • •

Meerkats greet each other every morning with chirps and nose touches.

• • •

Teamwork is the meerkat's superpower—they dig and forage together.

• • •

The alpha female leads the mob in single file when moving to a new home.

Some meerkats wear tiny radio collars for research missions that help scientists learn more about their habitats.

• • •

Each meerkat has a unique fur pattern, like a fingerprint.

• • •

Meerkats are sneaky and can sometimes swipe food from other animals' homes.

In the wild, meerkats live for around 12-14 years. They can live even longer in captivity because they don't have any predators.

• • •

Meerkats are super social and hate being alone.

• • •

Meerkats love taking quick naps during the day to recharge.

• • •

Meerkats use their calls to keep track of each other while exploring.

The landscape in Namibia, where meerkats live.

Meerkats can reach speeds of up to 32 km/h (20 mph)!

• • •

Meerkats have sharp, pointed teeth designed for gripping and tearing their prey. This is especially useful for catching insects, lizards, and small mammals.

• • •

Meerkats are an important part of the food chain. They help keep the insect population in check by eating pests.

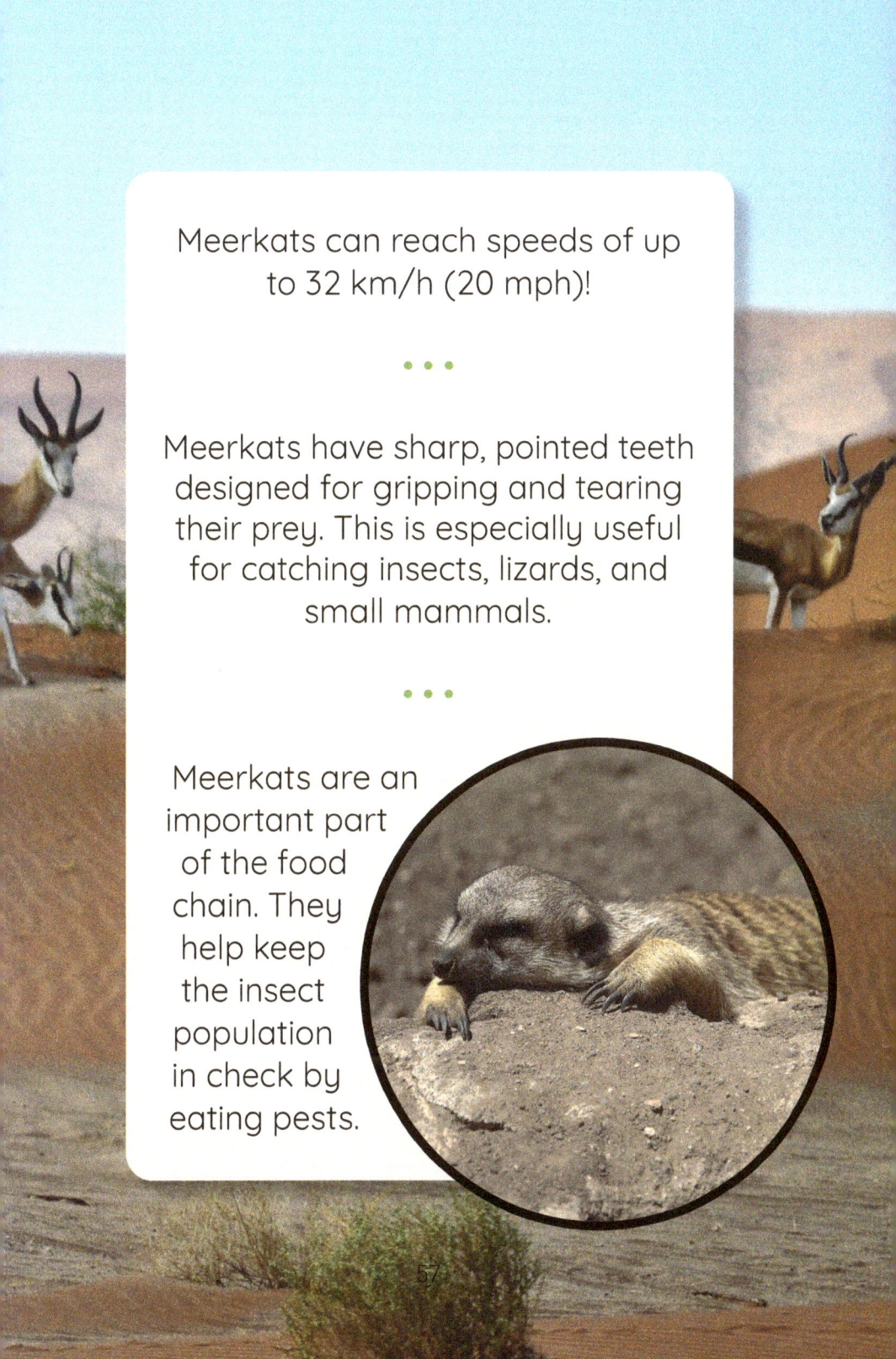

Meerkats can travel several kilometers a day while searching for food.

• • •

Meerkats are members of the mongoose family.

• • •

Male meerkats sometimes babysit while the females are out hunting.

• • •

Meerkats are around 29 cm (11 in) long with a 19 cm (7.4 in) tail.

• • •

Meerkats don't like the rain (they don't get much of it in the desert!), but they love munching on all the insects that come out afterwards.

Each meerkat has a unique face pattern, like a snowflake.

• • •

Meerkats are known to stand upright and face the sun in the mornings to warm up their bodies. This sunbathing behavior is essential as it helps them regulate their body temperature after a cold night.

• • •

Meerkats are always scanning the sky for eagles and other predators. It's a dangerous life for them!

• • •

Meerkats greet each other with nose-to-nose touches, like tiny high fives.

Meerkats have excellent eyesight with a wide field of view, allowing them to detect predators from a distance. They can spot birds of prey high in the sky and react quickly to the threat.

•••

Beetles are a favorite snack—crunchy and abundant!

•••

Meerkats have a unique way of marking their territory and deterring rivals using scent glands. They have anal scent glands that produce a strong-smell that they use to mark their burrows and territory boundaries.

The sentry duty among meerkats is not fixed; they each take turns, typically for about an hour at a time to ensure that everyone in the group gets a chance to rest.

...

Meerkats have been seen forming relationships with certain bird species, such as the drongo. The drongo acts as an extra pair of eyes for the meerkats, making loud calls when predators are near. In return, the birds benefit from easier access to insects stirred up by the foraging meerkats!

The Meerkat Quiz

Were you paying attention?! It's time to test your new meerkat knowledge!

1. What is a group of meerkats called?

2. Where do meerkats live?

3. Name three countries where meerkats can be found.

4   What is the role of the alpha female in a meerkat mob?

5   What do meerkats eat?

6   How do meerkats stay safe from predators?

7   What is a meerkat burrow?

8   How many different sounds can meerkats make?

9   What unique feature do meerkats have around their eyes to reduce sun glare?

10 What do meerkats do to warn each other about predators?

11 What kind of climate do meerkats live in?

12 True or False: Meerkats are solitary animals.

13 How do meerkats teach their young to hunt?

14 What is the primary function of a meerkat's tail?

15 Why do meerkats stand on their hind legs?

16 During what part of the day are meerkats most active?

17 What is one adaptation meerkats have for digging?

18 True or False: Meerkats can close their ears to keep out dirt while digging.

19 How long can a meerkat live in the wild?

20 How do meerkats keep their burrows cool?

21 What is one way meerkats communicate with each other?

Answers

HOW DID YOU DO?!

1. A mob.
2. In the deserts and grasslands of Southern Africa.
3. Botswana, Namibia, South Africa
4. She is the leader and the only female who has babies.
5. Insects, lizards, scorpions, and small mammals
6. They have sentinels who keep watch and alert the mob if there is danger.
7. An underground tunnel system where meerkats live.
8. Over 30 different sounds
9. Dark circles
10. They make alarm calls or bark loudly.
11. Hot and dry climate
12. False

13. Adult meerkats bring live prey to the pups to practice hunting.
14. To balance while standing upright.
15. To look out for predators and other dangers.
16. During the day (they are **diurnal**)
17. Long, strong claws
18. True
19. 12-14 years
20. By digging deep underground where it is cooler.
21. Through vocalizations, body language, and scent markings.

Meerkat

WORD SEARCH

```
F D S E N T I N E L C V
M C J H G D E F D S M J
A O M N I V O R E B E H
S C B P B D A Q W D E F
X C H U U F E J K T R D
C Q R I R P J S B N K R
A D G J R L M B E Q A G
Q E T Y O P Z G J R T F
T E Q A W X G U R E T B
W K A L A H A R I Z X N
G J D R F A B T D R F T
M T F D S E A L P H A D
```

Solution

		S	E	N	T	I	N	E	L		
M										M	
		O	M	N	I	V	O	R	E		E
		C	B		B	D					E
			H		U		E				R
			I	R			S				K
			R				E				A
			O	P				R			T
			W								T
	K	A	L	A	H	A	R	I			
						A	L	P	H	A	

Sources

NG, A. (2022). Meerkat Facts! Retrieved from https://www.natgeokids.com/uk/discover/animals/general-animals/meerkat-facts/

Britannica. (2024). Meerkats. Retrieved from https://kids.britannica.com/kids/article/meerkat/598989

Meerkat. (2024). Retrieved from https://nationalzoo.si.edu/animals/meerkat

Meerkat. (2024). Retrieved from https://animals.sandiegozoo.org/animals/meerkat

Kalahari Research Centre. (2024). Retrieved from https://kalahariresearchcentre.org/

Group Decision Making in Meerkats (2011). Retrieved from https://www.researchgate.net/publication/225280055_Group_decision-making_in_meerkats_Suricata_suricatta_-_PhD_thesis

Hemsworth, P. H. (2014). A multi-enclosure study investigating the behavioural response of meerkats to zoo visitors. Retrieved from https://www.sciencedirect.com/science/article/abs/pii/S0168159114001154

Teaching in Wild Meerkats (2006). Retrieved from https://www.researchgate.net/publication/6944406_Teaching_in_Wild_Meerkats

Garget, J. (2021). Monitoring the Meerkats of the Kalahari. Retrieved from https://www.cam.ac.uk/stories/meerkats

Proyectran. (2023). Loro Parque en redes. Retrieved from https://www.loroparque.com/en/datasheet-animals-meerkats/

Care For Us (Meerkat) (2024). Retrieved from https://wildwelfare.org/wp-content/uploads/Care-for-us-Meerkat.pdf

Trimarchi, M. (2008). How Meerkats Work. Retrieved from https://animals.howstuffworks.com/mammals/meerkats1.htm

Lewis, S. (n.d.). Meerkat. Retrieved from https://animalia.bio/index.php/meerkat

Kalahari Desert. (2024). Retrieved from https://en.wikipedia.org/wiki/Kalahari_Desert

Meerkat Care. (2024). Retrieved from https://www.rvc.ac.uk/Media/Default/Beaumont%20Sainsbury%20Animal%20Hospital/documents/Caring-for-your-meerkat%20Oct%202019.pdf

Mongoose, Meerkat, & Fossa (Herpestidae/ Eupleridae) Care Manual. (n.d.). Retrieved from https://nagonline.net/2510/mongoose-meerkat-fossa-herpestidaeeupleridae-care-manual/

Meerkat facts that will amaze your kids. (n.d.). Retrieved from https://tropicalworld.leeds.gov.uk/keepers-log/meerkat-facts-that-will-amaze-your-kids

DiLonardo, M. J. (2020). 11 Things You Didn't Know About Meerkats. Retrieved from https://www.treehugger.com/things-you-didnt-know-about-meerkats-4863935

Meerkat. (2024). Retrieved from https://kids.nationalgeographic.com/animals/mammals/facts/meerkat

That's all, folks!

As we reach the end of our exciting adventure through the wild world of meerkats, we hope you've enjoyed discovering these adorable creatures as much as we've loved bringing their stories to you.

Your thoughts are incredibly valuable to us, so we would be over the moon if you could **leave a review** wherever you picked up this book.

Your insights and experiences will help other young animal lovers uncover the wonderful world of meerkats and inspire us to create more content for you.

Thank you for being part of our meerkat mob!

ALSO BY JENNY KELLETT

 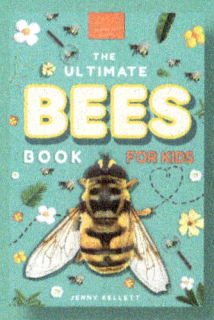 

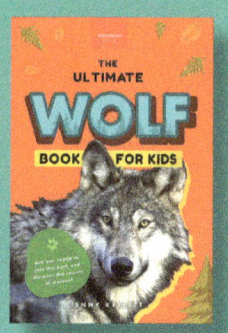 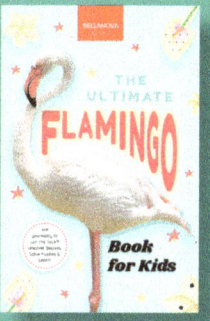 

... and more!

Available at
www.bellanovabooks.com
and all major online bookstores.

www.ingramcontent.com/pod-product-compliance
Lightning Source LLC
LaVergne TN
LVHW050136080526
838202LV00061B/6502